THE GROSSE ADVENTURES™

TROUBLE AT TWILIGHT CAVE

STINKY

STAN

by Annie Auerbach

manga**chapters**™

visit us at www.abdopublishing.com

Reinforced library bound edition published in 2009 by Spotlight, a division of ABDO
Publishing Group, 8000 West 78th Street, Edina, Minnesota 55439. This edition
reprinted by arrangement with TOKYOPOP Inc. www.tokyopop.com

Author	Annie Auerbach
Illustrator	Jamar Nicholas
Design and Layout	Courtney H. Geter
Cover Design	Anne Marie Horne
Senior Editor	Nicole Monastirsky
Digital Imaging Manager	Chris Buford
Pre-Press Supervisor	Erika Terriquez
Art Director	Anne Marie Horne
Production Manager	Elisabeth Brizzi

Cataloging-in-Publication Data

Auerbach, Annie.
  Trouble at Twilight Cave / written by Annie Auerbach ; illustrated by Jamar Nicholas.
    p. cm. -- (The Grosse Adventures ; bk. 3)
  "A TOKYOPOP, Inc. Manga Chapter."
Summary: Stinky and Stan finally have become full-fledged members of the Buzzardsd
and are headed to Spruce Mountain for a camping trip! When the boys meeet another
"troop" looking to collect their own achievement patches, will Stinky and Stan be able
to protect themselves?
  [1. Camping--Fiction. 2. Big Foot--Exhibitions--Fiction. 3. Flatulence--Fiction. 4.
Brothers--Fiction. 5. Twins--Fiction. 6. Humorous stories.] I. Jamar Nicholas, ill. II.
Title.
PZ7.A9118Goo 2007
[Fic]--dc22

For the real Buzzards: Chris, Peter, Shane, and Dan. And for Russ, who named them.

—A.A.

CONTENTS

THE BUZZARDS HAVE LANDED

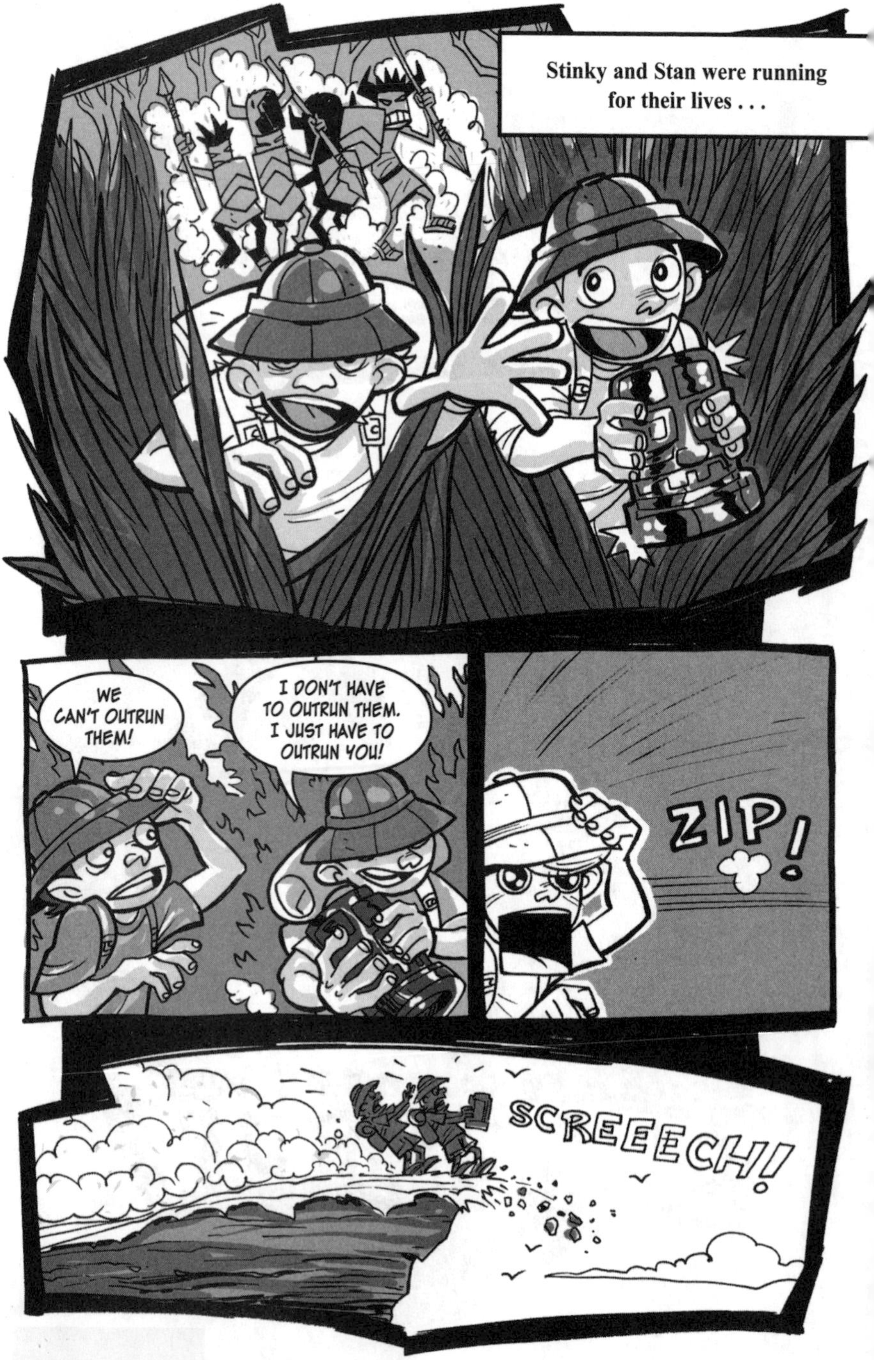

Stinky and Stan were running for their lives . . .
WE CAN'T OUTRUN THEM!
I DON'T HAVE TO OUTRUN THEM. I JUST HAVE TO OUTRUN YOU!
ZIP!
SCREEECH!

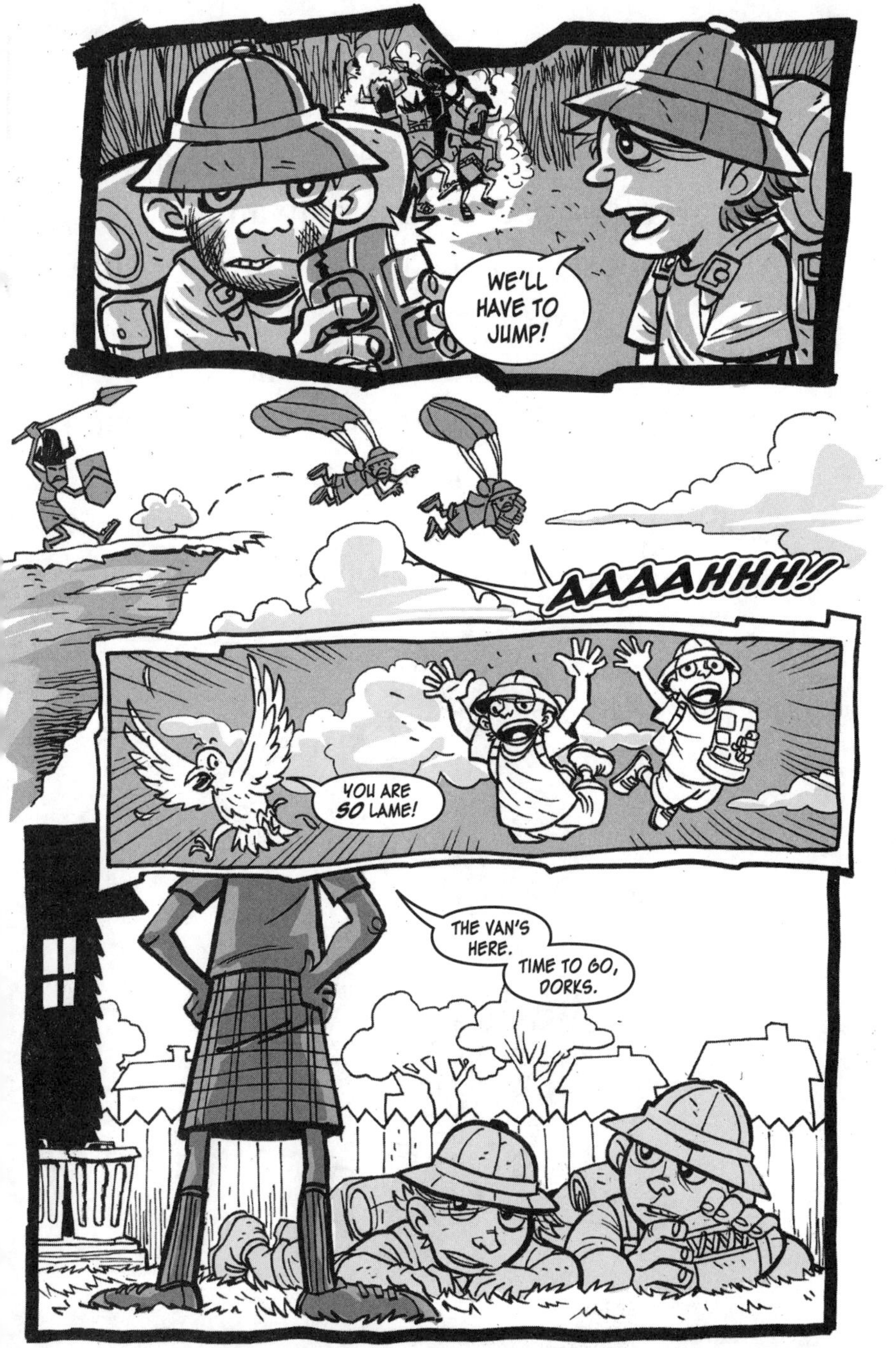
WE'LL HAVE TO JUMP!
AAAAHHH!
YOU ARE SO LAME!
THE VAN'S HERE.
TIME TO GO, DORKS.

"Are we there yet, sir?" Stan called out from the back of the minivan.

"Almost!" barked Mr. Hardbrickle from the driver's seat.

The six restless Wilderness Boys from Troop 768 were so excited about the upcoming camping trip that they could barely sit still in their seats. Mr. Hardbrickle, their Wilderness Leader,

made a right turn and drove up a dirt road. At the top was a campsite sign. Mr. Hardbrickle pulled into the parking lot.

"All right, troops! We're here!" he announced, turning the engine off.

"Hooray!" cheered the boys.

Eager to stretch their legs after the long drive, the boys piled out of the van. They were surrounded by tall trees, clean

air, and the peak of Spruce Mountain above.

"This place looks awesome!" said Stan. "I can't wait to go exploring!"

"Yeah!" agreed Stinky. "This is going to be such a great weekend!"

Click. Click. Click.

The brothers turned to see their friend Eugene Clunkenheimer already busy snapping pictures.

"Stand over there and smile," Eugene said to Stinky and Stan. "And no farting, or my lens will fog up!"

Stinky and Stan laughed. The Grosse brothers were known for their extreme farting abilities: Stinky's farts were silent and violent, while Stan's were loud and proud.

"Troops!" called Mr. Hardbrickle. "Unload the gear! Double-time to the campsite! Hut! Hut!" Mr. Hardbrickle was a retired army sergeant. Sometimes the boys weren't sure if *he* remembered he was actually retired.

"Yes, sir!" replied the boys.

On the short hike from the parking lot to the campsite, each troop member carried a backpack with a sleeping bag and tent.

Like most other Wilderness Boys, they had picked out a nickname. Instead of going for popular names like the Scorpions or the Eagles, the boys had called their troop the Buzzards. They had a secret handshake and took a special oath. They proudly sang their troop song during the hike:

> *Buzzards! Buzzards!*
> *Carrion's our feast!*
> *We eat both*
> *Man and beast!*
> *Yaaaaaay, Buzzards!*

"Troops! Fall in!" commanded Mr. Hardbrickle when they reached the campsite. "It's time you hear the ground rules."

The boys suppressed groans. Their troop leader loved rules—both making them and keeping them.

"Rule number one: all food must be strung from a tree or put in one of the lockers," began Mr. Hardbrickle. "These woods can be dangerous. Bears and—"

"There are bears here?!" Eugene worried out loud.

"Clunkenheimer! No talking when I'm talking!" said Mr. Hardbrickle. "That's rule number two."

Eugene looked down at his feet. He made a secret wish that the weekend would be bear-free.

"Rule number three: no one is to go near the Twilight Cave," continued the troop leader. "It is unsafe and I don't want to waste my weekend having to rescue any of you."

Stinky and Stan exchanged a quick glance. How exciting that cave sounded!

"If I find out that any of you go near there," said Mr. Hardbrickle, "you will spend the rest of the weekend shining my boots with your toothbrush!"

Stinky and Stan looked at each other. Maybe avoiding the cave would be best!

Then Mr. Hardbrickle ordered the boys to set up their tents and organize the campsite. Stinky and Stan took out their tent and sleeping bags. Two of the other troop members, Zach Linden and Colton Russell, took care of securing the food in an empty bear locker.

Eugene unpacked his camping gear and immediately put on bug repellent. He was terrified of getting bitten or stung. He lathered his arms and face with the stuff.

Then Eugene sneezed . . . and sneezed
. . . and sneezed. He was allergic to the
bug repellent! He grabbed a towel and
used it to wipe off the goop.

"Whew!" said Eugene, when he finally
stopped sneezing.

Bzzzt!

"Ow!" he cried.
He got stung!
"Argh!" he exclaimed.

Totally freaked out, he went to see if any of the other boys had a different brand he could borrow.

Meanwhile, Grñpæk Yvlåöqçkn, a foreign exchange student who no one could understand, was looking a little bewildered. It was obvious he had never been camping before. He set about trying to put his tent together, but he wasn't having much success. Before long, the only thing he *was* successful at was accidentally wrapping himself up in the tent like a mummy.

Just then, Mr. Hardbrickle happened to walk by.

"Qqw yvvn pttz ksp?" Grñpæk asked Mr. Hardbrickle.

But the troop leader had no idea what he was saying. "Uh . . . get that tent up!" he ordered and walked over to where Stan was setting up his tent.

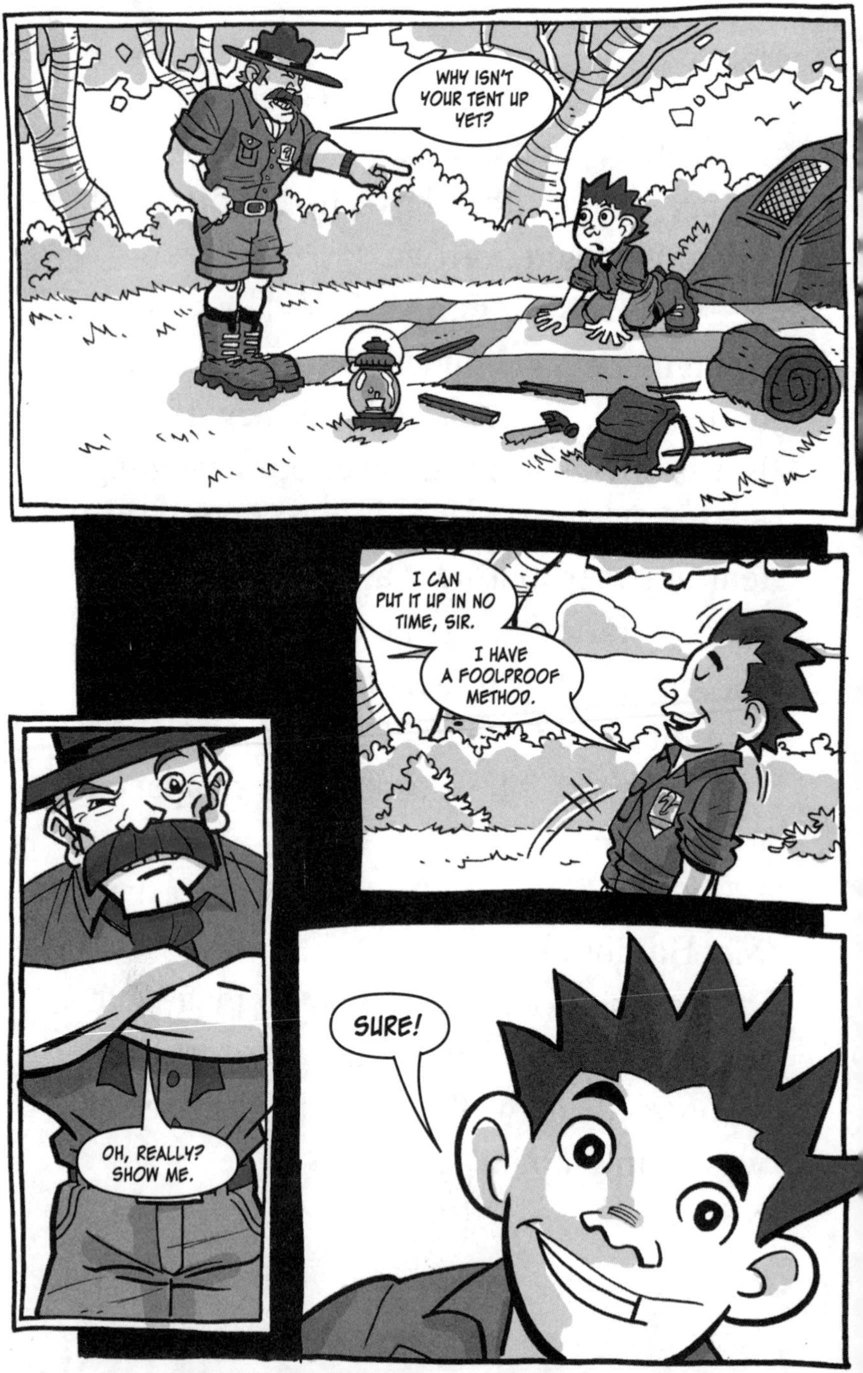
WHY ISN'T YOUR TENT UP YET?
I CAN PUT IT UP IN NO TIME, SIR.
I HAVE A FOOLPROOF METHOD.
OH, REALLY? SHOW ME.
SURE!

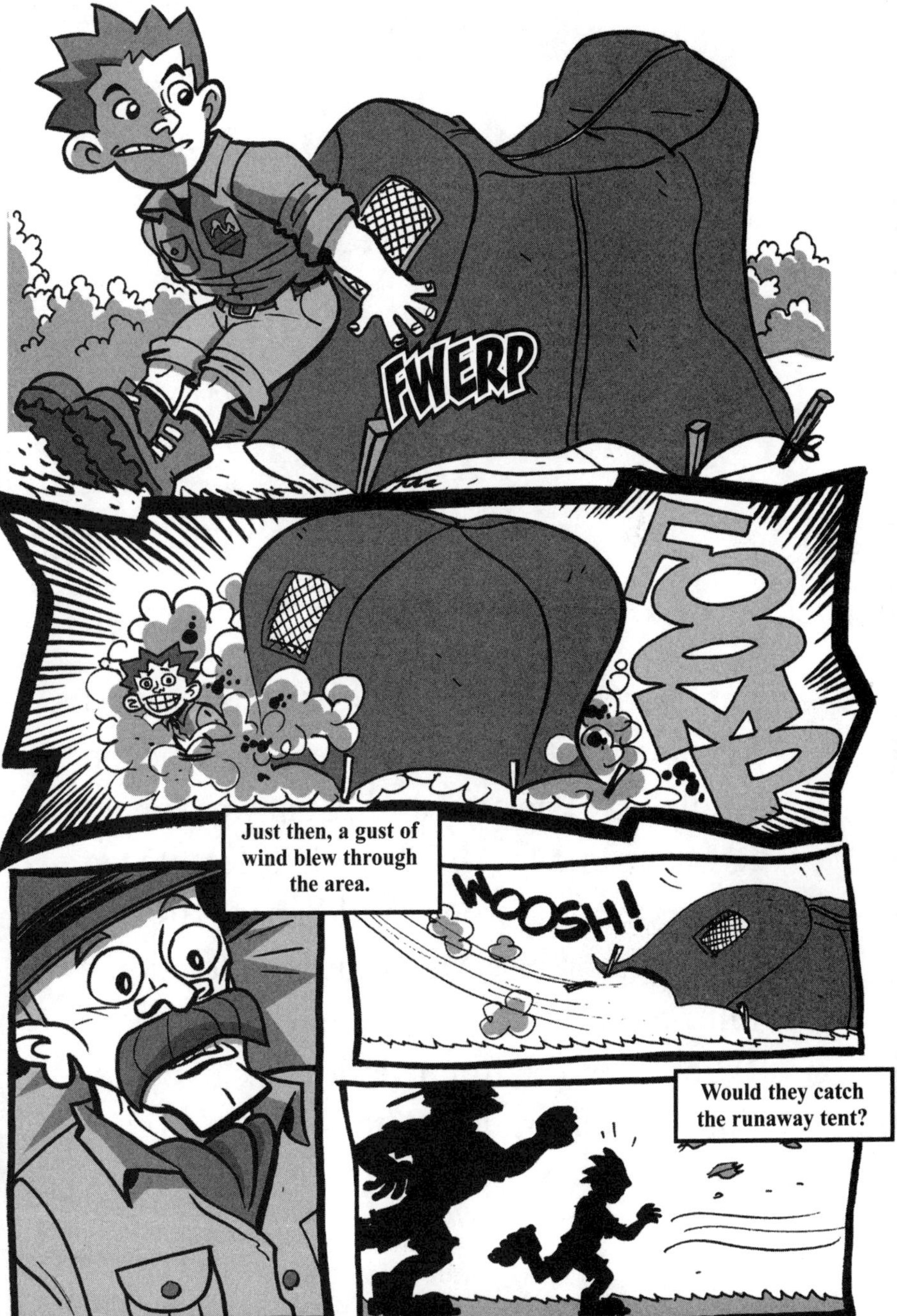
FWERP
FOOMP
Just then, a gust of wind blew through the area.
WOOSH!
Would they catch the runaway tent?

CHAPTER TWO

WILD ANIMALS AFOOT

Mr. Hardbrickle and Stan recovered the runaway tent. It blew pretty far, and the whole way back to camp, Stan was forced to listen to Mr. Hardbrickle's lecture on the duties of a proper Wilderness Boy.

It was clear Mr. Hardbrickle didn't think Stan had been studying the rulebook. When they finally made it back to camp, Stan was so relieved to see his brother and the others.

"I was going to gather some deadwood for our campfire," Stinky said to Stan. "Do you want to come?"

Stan couldn't say "yes" fast enough. He practically ran out of the there to get away from Mr. Hardbrickle.

"What's going on?" Stinky asked.

"Hardbrickle's driving me crazy," said Stan. "Then again, I guess I should have just put the tent up the normal way, instead of farting into it."

"Yeah, but where's the fun in that?" Stinky said.

Stan grinned. It was cool to have a brother who just understood.

In a shady area, the boys found some dead branches and collected them to bring back to camp.

Just then, in the middle of the woods, the brothers came face to face with some wild animals!

Actually, it was just some girls from school: Penelope, Tiffanie, Steffanie, Kim-Yun, and Lauren. Their Wilderness Girls troop was called the Poppies.

"What are you doing here?" asked Stinky.

"We could ask you the same question," said Tiffanie. Then she thought for a moment. "And we are. Asking, that is."

Penelope rolled her eyes. Then she looked at Stinky's and Stan's uniforms.

"Oh, no," she said. "Don't tell me you goobers are camping here. This is *our* area."

"Who made you boss of the woods?" said Stinky. "We have just as much a right to be here as you." He looked at one of the patches on Penelope's uniform. "You're called the *Poopies?*"

"Poppies! We're the Poppies!" exclaimed Penelope, outraged.

"Really? You don't strike me as the

outdoorsy types," said Stan.

Steffanie sighed. "Well, if you must know, we're on a Wilderness Girls weekend. We tried to get it to take place at the mall, but our leader, Mrs. O'Brien, wouldn't let us."

"What a shame," said Stinky. "I guess you'll have to rough it this weekend. How will the mall survive without you?"

"Shut up, Stinky," said Penelope. She noticed the Buzzards patch on his uniform. "The Buzzards? That figures. Buzzards only like gross, disgusting things."

"Well, we are talking to you, aren't we?" chimed in Stan.

Penelope pursed her lips together. "Just stay out of our part of the woods," she warned.

"We'd be glad to," said Stinky, as the two groups headed their separate ways.

CHAPTER THREE

BRRR!!!

The weekend camping trip was really important to the Buzzards for a very specific reason: they all hoped to earn achievement patches. The more achievement patches a troop member earned, the sooner he could advance to the next level of Wilderness Boy.

Now, these were no ordinary patches. Sure, there were the typical ones like an Archery Patch or a Canoeing Patch. But the Wilderness Boys also had patches that were, well, unique. There was an Animal Poop Patch, a Letting Bugs Crawl on Your Face Patch, and even a Staring Contest Patch.

One of the patches that could be earned during the camping weekend was the Freeze Your Butt Off patch. For this one, Mr. Hardbrickle and the Buzzards had hiked to a nearby stream.

staring contest

"Atten-hut!" said Mr. Hardbrickle. "Prepare to plunge!"

The boys looked at one another. Nobody moved. Nobody wanted to be first.

"NOW!" barked Mr. Hardbrickle.

"Yes, sir!" replied the boys, a little scared. They instantly stripped down to their bathing suits.

To obtain this achievement patch, you had to get into the freezing water up to your waist and stay there for five minutes.

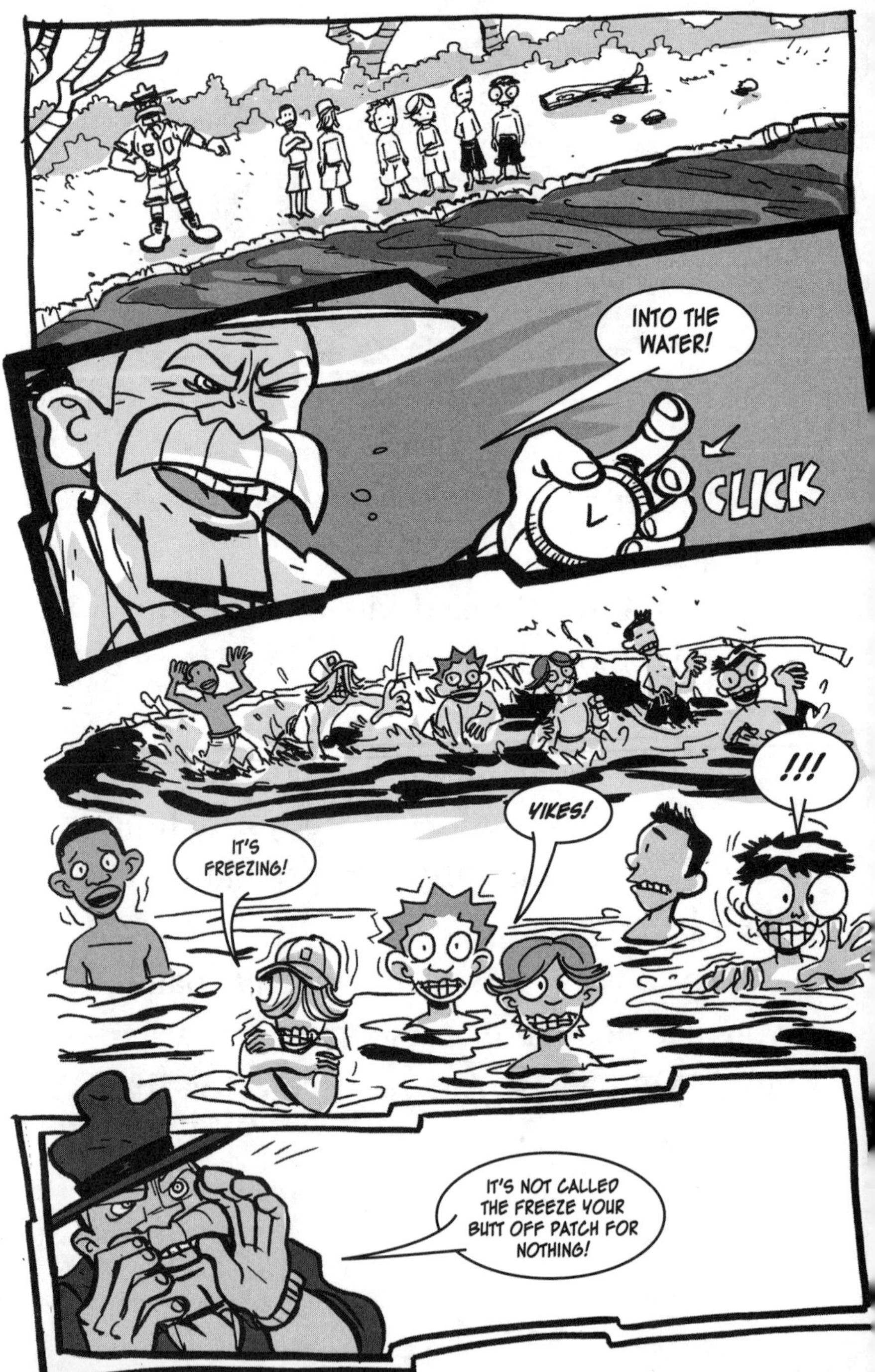
INTO THE WATER!
CLICK
IT'S FREEZING!
YIKES!
!!!
IT'S NOT CALLED THE FREEZE YOUR BUTT OFF PATCH FOR NOTHING!

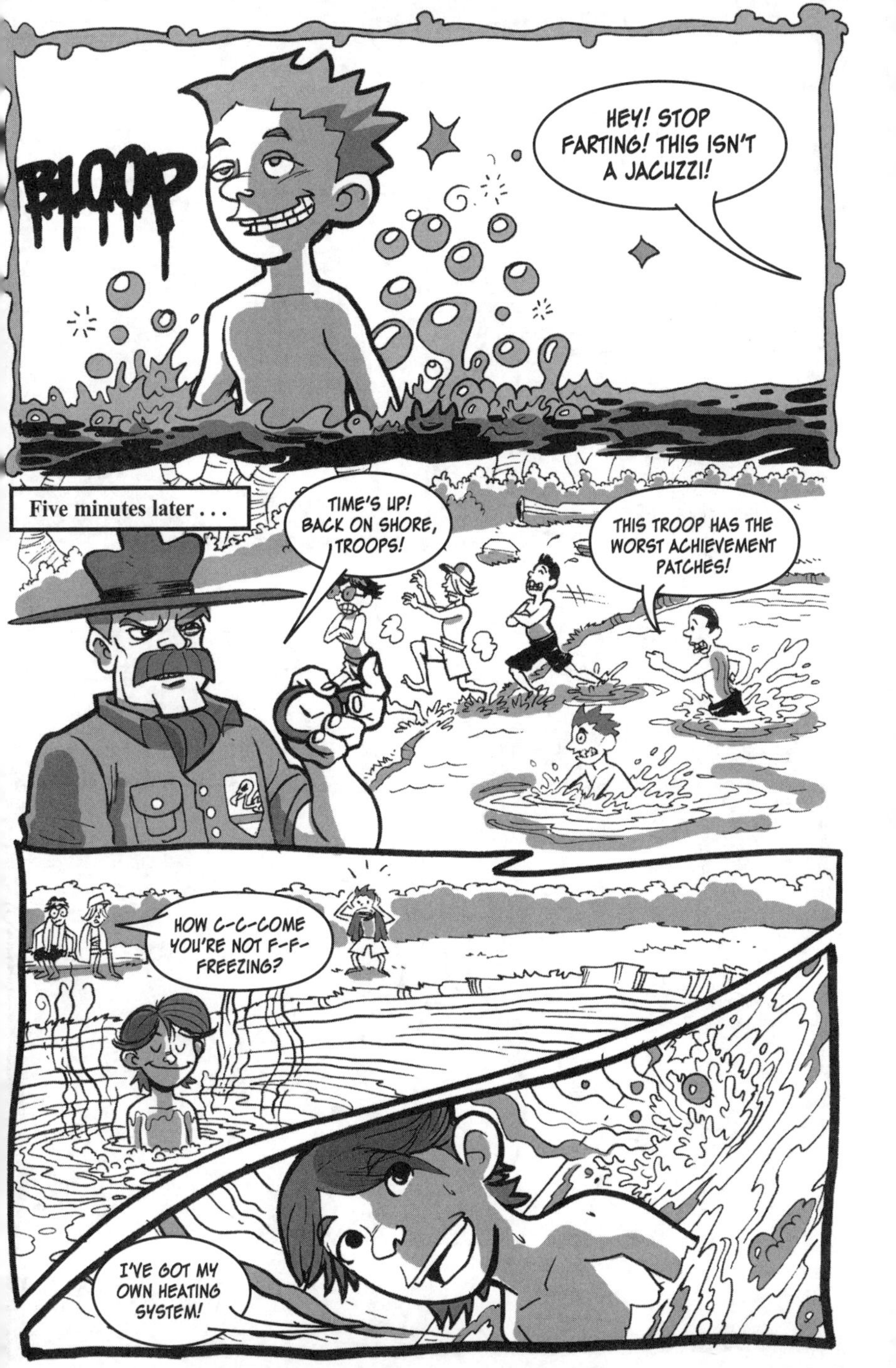
BLOOP
HEY! STOP FARTING! THIS ISN'T A JACUZZI!
Five minutes later . . .
TIME'S UP! BACK ON SHORE, TROOPS!
THIS TROOP HAS THE WORST ACHIEVEMENT PATCHES!
HOW C-C-COME YOU'RE NOT F-F-FREEZING?
I'VE GOT MY OWN HEATING SYSTEM!

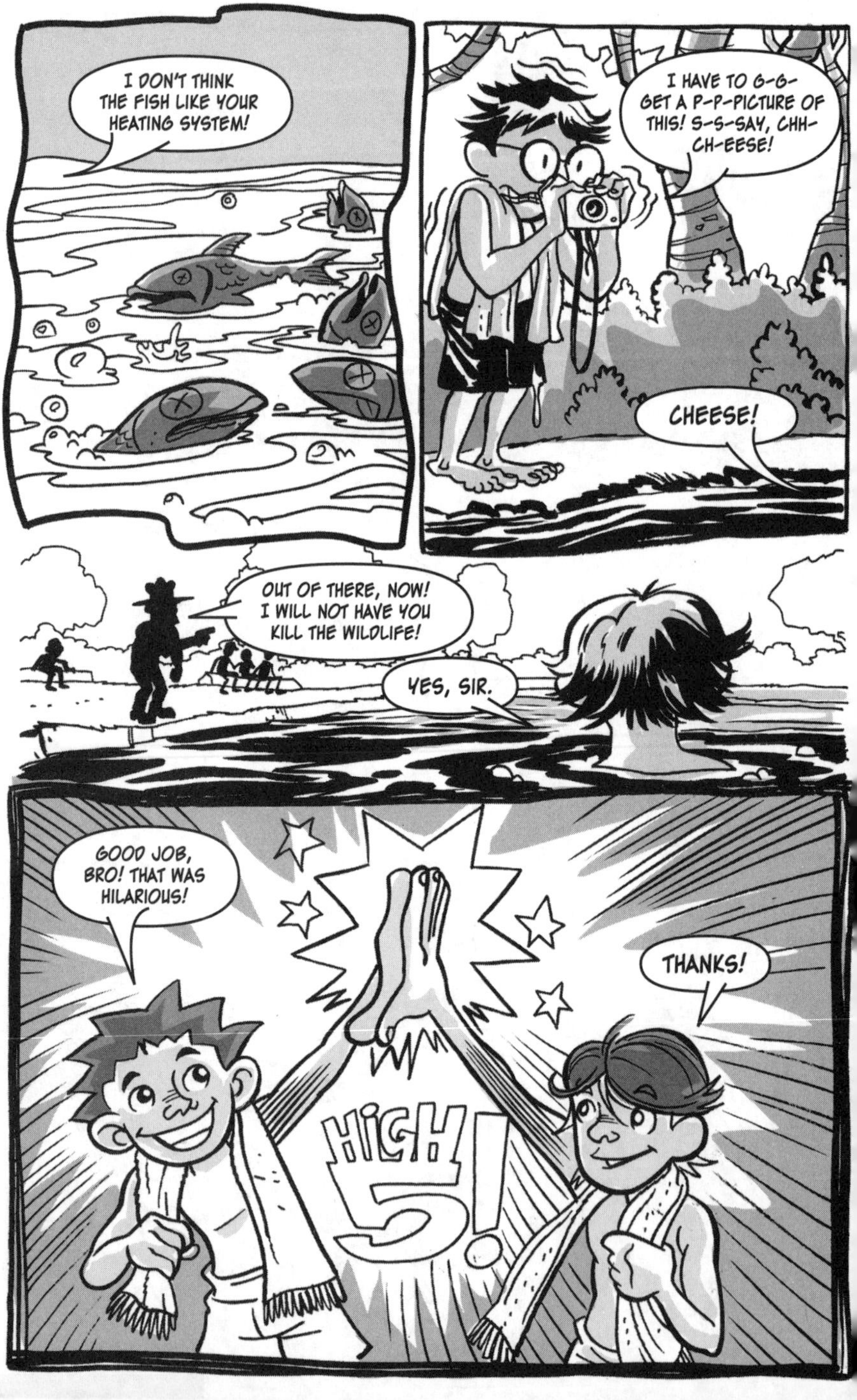
I DON'T THINK THE FISH LIKE YOUR HEATING SYSTEM!
I HAVE TO G-G-GET A P-P-PICTURE OF THIS! S-S-SAY, CHH-CH-EESE!
CHEESE!
OUT OF THERE, NOW! I WILL NOT HAVE YOU KILL THE WILDLIFE!
YES, SIR.
GOOD JOB, BRO! THAT WAS HILARIOUS!
THANKS!
HIGH 5!

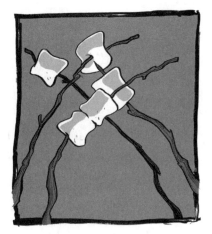

CHAPTER FOUR
A SCARY STORY

The now-numb boys were overjoyed to get out of the stream and head back to the camp. The gasping fish were pretty happy to see them leave, too. And, in case you're wondering, the boys did earn their patches. Of course, being able to put on warm clothes was almost better than getting the patch. Almost. A patch is a patch, after all.

Sitting around the roaring campfire, the boys ate hot dogs for dinner.

"Achoo! Achoo! ACHOO!"

Eugene couldn't stop sneezing. Although he was allergic to a lot of things, those sneezes were probably from the chill he got from being in the ice-cold water.

"Be careful, Eugene," said Stan. "You might put out the fire if you sneeze hard enough!"

"Sorry, guys," Eugene replied. "I think I'm allergic to camping."

"Hey, is it marshmallow time yet?" Colton asked. He loved roasting marshmallows over an open fire.

"Yes, it is, troops," said Mr. Hardbrickle. He passed around a large bag of marshmallows. When Grñpæk got the bag, he took a handful and popped them into his mouth.

"You're not supposed to eat them yet!" Mr. Hardbrickle barked. He motioned to the other boys who were putting their marshmallows onto the end of their sticks and placing them near the fire.

"Wqqzx gbpo xcxzsp," Grñpæk said, slightly embarrassed. He tried to chew and swallow all the ones in his mouth. Then, of course, he needed *another* marshmallow for his stick!

As they roasted marshmallows, the boys sang a few songs.

Suddenly, Grñpæk exclaimed, "Vvlkp opxxz mnmpyq!"

"What's he saying?" asked Stinky.

"I don't know," said Eugene. "Hey, G, what's the matter?"

He called Grñpæk "G" since his name was so hard to pronounce.

"Vvlkp opxxz mnmpyq!!!" Grñpæk said again. He pointed to the marshmallow on the end of his stick.

Stan started to laugh. "It exploded!"

Sure enough, Grñpæk left his marshmallow in the fire too long. It had caught fire, expanded, and burned until it was three times the size of the original. And as tasty as charcoal.

"It's okay, G," said Zach. "You're just a marshmallow newbie. It takes a long time to be a pro at this."

"Yeah, you're a pro, all right," said Stinky with a laugh. "You'd better put yours out!"

Zach quickly grabbed his stick out of the fire. The marshmallow had caught fire, so he quickly blew it out. Embarrassed, his face became as red as the flames of the fire.

"Hey! Do you guys want to hear a scary story?" Stinky asked the group. There was only one thing Stinky liked more than being scared: scaring others.

"Yeah!" the other boys replied. "Let's hear it!"

Stinky grabbed a flashlight, put it under his chin, and turned it on. The light created a creepy shadow—perfect for a scary story in the middle of the woods . . .

Once there was a young man who inherited a huge mansion from an uncle who had recently died. When the man moved in a few weeks later, he got a phone call. The voice on the other end said, "I am the Vinder Viper. I will be there in two weeks!"

Then the line went dead.

A week passed with no calls, until one night. The phone rang around 7 P.M.

"I am the Vinder Viper. I will be there in one week!" said the voice and hung up.

This made the man very nervous. Was something coming for him? What should he do? The man went on the Internet to look up "snakes" and "Vinder Viper," but he found nothing.

Five days later, the phone rang again. "I am the Vinder Viper. I will be there tomorrow!"

The man was really worried now.

The next day, the phone rang. "I am the Vinder Viper. I will be there in one hour!"

The young man finally snapped. Scared out of his mind, he tried to leave, but his car battery was dead. He was trapped! He called 911. The police were on their way.

Soon there was a knock on the door. The man opened the door a crack and asked, "Is that the police?"

A small, German man replied, "No. I am the vinder viper. I come every month to vipe your vindows."

All the boys groaned, which was high praise around a campfire.

"That was awful!" said Colton.

"Bmpq wwxz!" added Grñpæk.

"Thank you," said Stinky, grinning. "Thank you very much."

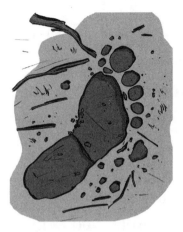

CHAPTER FIVE
THE LEGEND

The boys were still groaning from Stinky's scary story when someone else spoke up.

"I have a story for you," the voice said.

The boys were surprised. The "voice" belonged to Mr. Hardbrickle!

"Cool!" said Stan.

"Tell it!" said Stinky.

"Are you sure?" asked the troop leader. "It might be too scary for some of you," he said, looking right at Eugene.

Eugene's face flashed with fear. Then he sat up straight and puffed out his chest. "Let's hear it," he said.

Mr. Hardbrickle gave a small smile, cleared his throat, and began his tale . . .

There is a legend that lives deep in these woods.

A legend of a creature that hunts in these parts.

A legend of a creature called Bigfoot.

Over twelve feet tall with massive hands and feet, he leaves giant footprints wherever he goes.

He is covered from head to toe with hair and is so strong that he can snap a tree in half with only one hand. It is said that he lives in the Twilight Cave.

"*The* Twilight Cave?" interrupted Eugene.

"What's the matter, Eugene? Scared?" teased Zach.

Eugene quickly caught himself. "Uh . . . no . . . I was just clarifying. You know, to make sure it wasn't some other Twilight Cave."

Zach snickered. "Oh, good. Thanks."

"You want to hear the rest of the story or not?" Mr. Hardbrickle said to the group.

"Yes! Sorry, sir," Eugene said.

"Now, where was I?" said Mr. Hardbrickle. "Oh, yes. The cave . . ."

The Forestry Department has forbidden anyone to go into the cave. They say it's because of falling rocks and hidden pitfalls. But the real reason is because that's where Bigfoot lives. It is said that dozens of Wilderness Boy skeletons litter the ground.

Hikers and campers have glimpsed Bigfoot over the years and have taken some blurry photos, but no one can prove they're real.

There are stories of Bigfoot smashing ranger stations to pieces, scaring hikers off cliffs, or sneaking into campsites— much like this one—and stealing boys and girls right from their tents. They disappear without a sound and are never heard from again . . .

Mr. Hardbrickle looked around the campsite. All the boys were so scared that they were holding their breath. The troop leader smiled to himself.

"Time to hit the sack," he announced and dumped a bucket of water onto the fire, turning it into a big cloud of hissing steam. "Sleep well, troops."

As the boys walked into their tents, Eugene whispered to Stinky and Stan. "Sleep well? After that story? Is he kidding?"

"Oh, come on," said Stinky. "It's just a story."

Stan agreed. "It isn't real," he told Eugene. "But, if it is, and Bigfoot tries to take you in the middle of the night, just holler and we'll come rescue you."

Eugene looked down at his feet, a little embarrassed. Then he turned and said, "Thanks, guys."

"No problem," said Stinky as he and his brother headed toward the tent they shared and crawled into their sleeping bags.

"Too bad Eugene is scared," said Stan.

"Yeah," said Stinky. "I'm glad we don't get scared by stories like that. Bigfoot? Come on. That's just silly."

"Totally silly," agreed Stan.

But secretly, each boy slept with his flashlight in his hand . . . just in case.

CHAPTER SIX
ANIMAL PRANKS

Around two o'clock in the morning, Stinky woke up with an idea.

"Hey, Stan, wake up," he whispered to his brother.

"What is it?" Stan yawned. Then he rolled over and went back to sleep.

Stinky nudged him. "I think we should go scare the girls!"

That was all Stan needed to hear. "Why didn't you say that in the first place? *Now* I'm awake!" he said and got out of his sleeping bag.

"Great!" Stinky said. "Let's get the others."

Stinky and Stan made sure that Mr. Hardbrickle was sleeping soundly; then they went to round up the other boys. In no time at all, the six boys were armed with flashlights and headed into the woods . . .

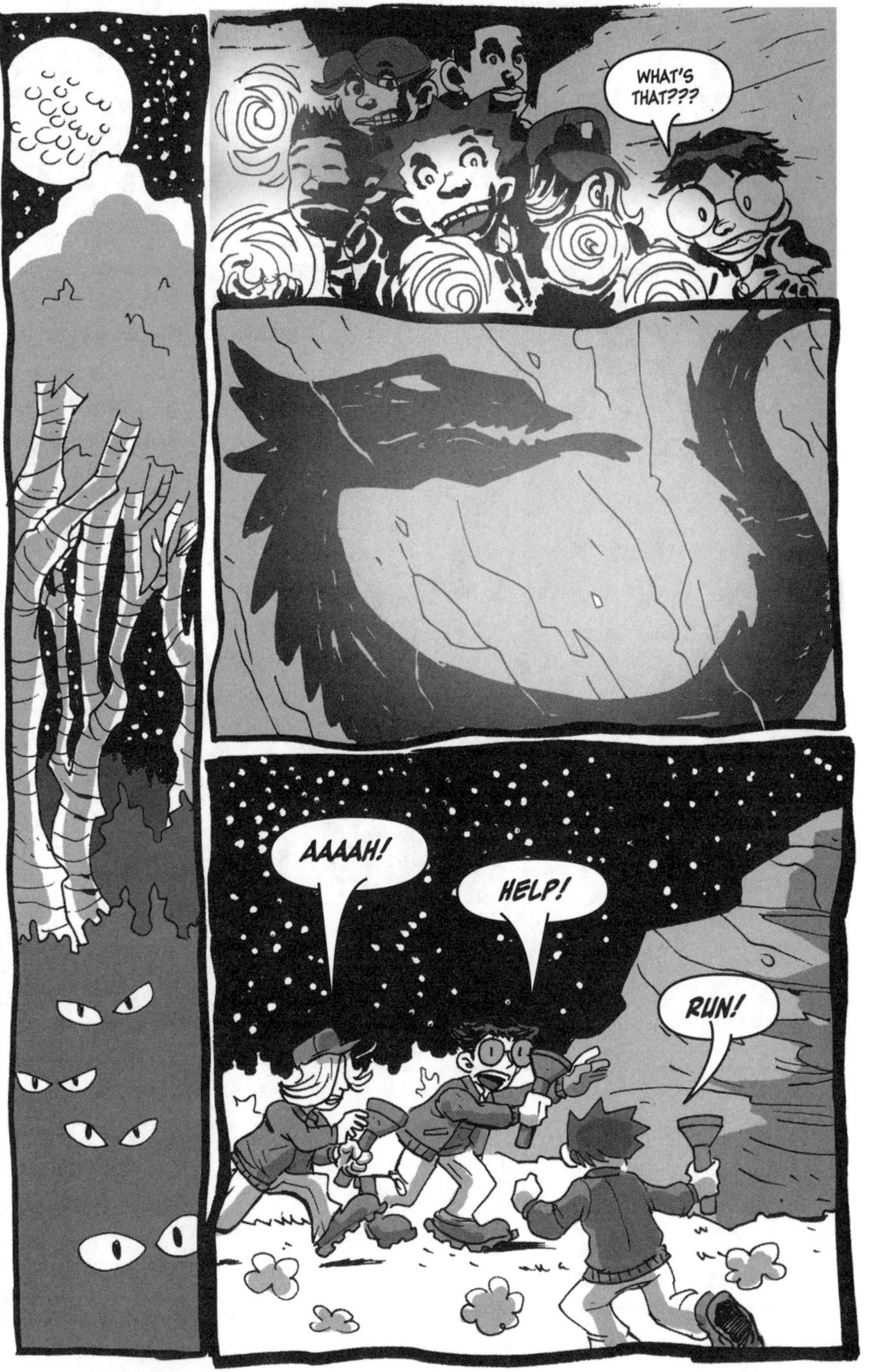
WHAT'S THAT???
AAAAH!
HELP!
RUN!

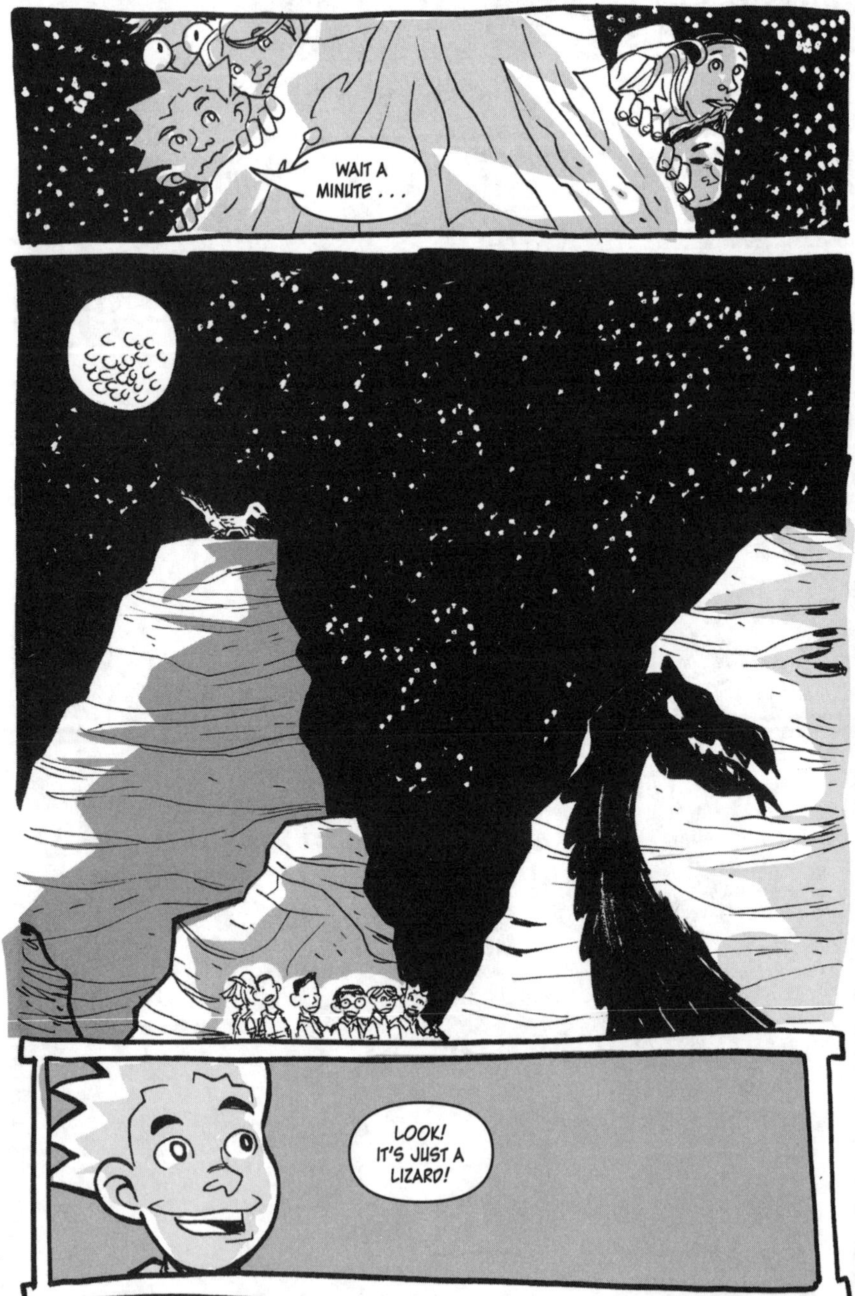
WAIT A MINUTE . . .
LOOK! IT'S JUST A LIZARD!

"That was so lame!" said Colton.

"Yeah," agreed Eugene. "I can't believe you were scared of a little lizard."

Colton looked at Eugene. "If I remember correctly, *you* were pretty scared yourself."

"Well, uh, I, uh," stammered Eugene. "I was just, uh—"

"Hey! That lizard gave me a great idea. Grab some tree branches from the ground and I'll tell you the idea on the way," said an excited Stinky.

Before long, the boys were at the girls' campsite. They made sure to be very quiet as they crept up to the girls' tents, using only the moonlight as their guide. Stan took two branches, placed them above his head, and looked back at his brother, who was ready with the flashlight.

Stinky looked over at Zach and Colton, who were holding their tree branches like

big, scary arms. They nodded at Stinky.
Stinky checked with Eugene and Grñpæk,
who were hunched down by another tent.
Everyone was ready for the Buzzard
Attack.

"One, two, three!" Stinky mouthed.

Everything happened at once. Stinky
turned on the flashlight, projecting monster-
shaped shadows onto the girls' tents.

Eugene and Grñpæk growled and
grunted, while shaking the tents.

Then came the high-pitched response: "AAAAAAAAHHHHHHHH!" The girls screamed in fear. They huddled together in their tents, not knowing what to do.

Stinky looked at Stan and grinned. The plan worked perfectly!

That is until the leader, Mrs. O'Brien, came running out of her tent. In white face cream, she looked scarier than the creatures the boys made up!

"RUN!" Stinky screamed.

The boys took off, running at lightning speed. It was a narrow escape, but all of them got out alive. What a close call!

Mrs. O'Brien found her flashlight and turned it on. She was relieved to see nothing there.

"It's all right, girls," she announced. "It's safe to come out."

The girls poked their heads out of their tents, looked around, and then filed out.

"That was so scary!" said Penelope.

"I saw a monster!" said Kim-Yun.

"I saw one of Santa's reindeer!" said Tiffanie.

The girls gave Tiffanie a puzzled look.

"Well . . . maybe not one of Santa's reindeer," said Tiffanie. "But it had antlers!"

"You can all go back to bed," said Mrs. O'Brien. "It's gone now, whatever it was."

"Or whomever," said Penelope, spotting something on the ground. She picked it up. It was a flashlight—with Eugene's name on it.

Penelope seethed. "I should have known it was them."

POPPIES

CHAPTER SEVEN

REVENGE OF THE POPPIES

The following morning, Stinky and Stan sat bolt upright in their tent.

"Is that a bugle?!" exclaimed Stinky. He covered his ears to try and block out the sound. It didn't work.

"Man, what time is it?" Stan said.

"Rise and shine!" Mr. Hardbrickle announced.

"Does this guy remember that this is not *actually* the army?" asked Stan.

The boys got out of their sleeping bags and began to get dressed. They could hear Mr. Hardbrickle coming.

"Hurry!" said Stinky.

With no time to spare, the boys finished putting on their clothes and jumped into their shoes. Just as Hardbrickle turned the corner, the boys closed their tent and stood at attention.

That's when they discovered the girls' revenge.

Stinky and Stan looked down to see that their shoes had been filled with peanut butter! It surrounded their feet, oozing out from the top.

"Yuck!" Stan said.

"What was that, soldier?" said Mr. Hardbrickle, getting right in his face.

"Uh . . . nothing, sir," replied Stan, standing at attention, despite the squishing sounds in his shoes.

Mr. Hardbrickle inspected each boy from head to toe. "Pull up those socks! Tie those shoes! Eugene—underwear goes on the inside of your shorts!"

Eugene looked down and flushed with embarrassment.

Then Mr. Hardbrickle noticed a distinct smell. A peanut-y smell. He looked at the boys' shoes and furrowed his brow.

"Troops! Why do you have peanut butter in your shoes?" he demanded.

"We don't know, sir!" replied the troop.

"You don't know why there's peanut butter in your shoes?" asked Mr. Hardbrickle.

"No, sir!" the troops said.

"I want that peanut butter out of your shoes by breakfast!" Mr. Hardbrickle commanded. "Company, dismissed!"

None of the boys could get all the peanut butter out. It was seriously sticky stuff, after all.

"The girls sure got us good," said Stinky over breakfast.

"How did they know it was us?" wondered Stan.

"Yeah," agreed Zach. "I thought we got out of there before anyone saw us."

Stinky looked at Eugene, who was being awfully quiet. "Eugene? You okay?"

"What? It wasn't me!" babbled Eugene. "I mean, I didn't mean to drop it. It was an accident—"

"Whoa! Slow down!" said Stan. "What are you talking about?"

Eugene gulped, realizing he just revealed too much. "Um . . . it's kind of a funny story . . ."

The other boys exchanged suspicious looks.

"Well, when the girls' leader came out last night," explained Eugene, "I got scared and accidentally dropped my flashlight."

"So?" asked Colton. "Why wouldn't they think it was one of theirs?"

"Or even a previous camper's?" added Stan.

"Uh . . . I'm sure you're going to laugh about this . . . in ten or twenty years," replied Eugene. "My, uh, name was on the flashlight."

"WHAT?!" said the boys at exactly the same time.

"Eugene, why is your name on everything?" asked Stan.

It was true. It was even on his underwear.

Eugene's face reddened. "It's my mother. She does it."

The boys groaned. "Well, that explains the peanut butter payback," said Stinky.

After breakfast, the boys split up to work on getting the patches they needed. Zach and Colton needed to get their

Forestry Patches and headed into the woods to identify trees.

Eugene needed to get his Animal Poop Patch. To earn the patch, he would have to identify different types of poop from all kinds of forest creatures.

"I think this might be worse than the Freeze Your Butt Off Patch," Eugene muttered to himself as he found some deer poop.

Grñpæk needed to get his Roots & Berries Patch. He headed toward a bush of berries and grabbed one. He was about to pop it into his mouth when he heard Mr. Hardbrickle yelling at him.

"STOP! Don't eat that! It's poisonous!"

Grñpæk immediately dropped the berry, shaking with fear. It was hard to tell which he was more frightened of: Mr. Hardbrickle or eating a poisonous berry.

Mr. Hardbrickle ran over to Grñpæk and tried to explain that he was just supposed to identify the berries, not eat them!

"Vjpww jlza tqpc?" asked Grñpæk.

Mr. Hardbrickle sighed. It was going to be a loooong morning.

Meanwhile, Stinky and Stan paired up. They each needed to earn a Bird Watching Patch. Grabbing a pair of binoculars, the brothers went into the forest.

"So, what birds do we need to find?" Stan asked his brother.

"A hawk, a sparrow, a swallow, a crossbill, and a woodpecker," said Stinky, reading from his notebook.

"Shh! Listen!" said Stan suddenly. He could hear rapid chirping. But was it one of the ones they needed to spot?

Using the binoculars, Stan confirmed it was a sparrow!

Stinky took a look, too. "Cool," he said, marking down the details in his notebook. "One down, four to go."

As the boys continued walking, they looked in the trees and all around them for the other birds. At one point, Stan saw something strange. It looked like a really big ape. He used the binoculars to try and see more clearly, but suddenly nothing was there. He thought maybe his eyes were playing tricks on him.

But were they?

CHAPTER EIGHT
DO YOU SEE WHAT I SEE?

Two hours later, the boys had already spotted a hawk and a crossbill.

"Now we just need the swallow and the woodpecker, and we're done," said Stinky.

But Stinky and Stan's mission came to a screeching halt when they ran smack into Penelope, Tiffanie, and Steffanie.

"Well, well, if it isn't the peanut butter bandits," said Stinky.

Penelope smiled. "Payback is sweet," she said. "Sorry we didn't have any jelly to go with it."

Steffanie pointed to the boys' shoes and giggled. "You got super chunky! You got creamy!"

Stan grimaced. "Did you just come here to gloat?" he asked.

"As much fun as it is to see you suffer, we actually need to spot some birds for our Bird Watching Patch," explained Penelope.

"Great," Stinky said, grumpily.

"Couldn't you use a different part of the forest?" asked Stan.

"Why should *we* leave?" said Tiffanie.

"That's right," said Penelope. "Besides, this is supposed to be the best area to spot woodpeckers."

Stinky pulled Stan aside. "If there are more of us looking, maybe we'll spot the birds faster," he whispered.

Stan nodded. "Good idea! Then we'd be done with this sooner."

The boys suggested the plan to work together, and soon the group was walking along the forest path, looking and listening for birds.

A few minutes later, Penelope heard a distinct sound.

"I think I hear a woodpecker!" she said and ran ahead of the group. She stood under a tree and pointed to a bird high in the branches above. Then the most shocking thing happened: a furry creature came out from behind a tree, grabbed Penelope, and ran into the woods!

CHAPTER NINE
A HAIRY SITUATION

"What was that?!?" cried Tiffanie.

"I think it might have been an ape," said Steffanie.

"I think it was a real live wookie!" said Stan.

"No," said Stinky quietly. "It was Bigfoot."

The others turned to him in shock.

"Do you actually think he's real?" asked Stan, stunned.

"Who else could it be?" replied Stinky. "He was furry and strong enough to pick up Penelope easily."

"But he wasn't really *that* tall," said Stan. "At least not as tall as Mr. Hardbrickle had described him."

"Yeah, that was weird," said Stinky.

"Hel-LO?" interrupted Tiffanie. "Our best friend has just been captured by a hairy beast. Do you think you could stop talking about how tall he was and help us figure out what to do?"

"Sorry. You're totally right," said Stinky. "Okay, well, the Bigfoot headed in the direction of the Twilight Cave. We should probably start there."

"The Twilight Cave?" said Stan. "No one's supposed to go in there! Remember what Mr. Hardbrickle said?"

"He's right," said Tiffanie. "You know, maybe we should go back and tell our troop leaders first. I'm sure they'll know what to do."

Stinky and Stan were stunned. Tiffanie had actually come up with a good idea. It might have been the first one ever. So the boys and girls split up and ran back to their camps as fast as possible.

When Stinky and Stan found Mr. Hardbrickle, he was just sitting around reading.

"Mr. Hardbrickle!" the boys shouted. "We saw Bigfoot!"

The troop leader laughed. "Oh, did you? Was he fishing for the Loch Ness Monster?"

"What? No! We saw him in the forest!" Stan said urgently.

"Settle down, now, settle down," said Mr. Hardbrickle. "Bigfoot is just a legend. He's not real. I think your imaginations have run a bit wild."

"No! It was Bigfoot!" insisted Stinky. "And he took—"

"That's enough," Mr. Hardbrickle said. "Shouldn't you be working on getting your achievement patches instead of making up crazy stories?"

The boys walked away very frustrated. They knew what they had seen. They also knew that they would have to save Penelope on their own. But that didn't mean they weren't scared.

"Remember how Hardbrickle said the cave was littered with Wilderness Boy skeletons? What if Bigfoot grabs us, too?" worried Stan.

"We're just going to have to outsmart him," replied Stinky. "I don't know how, but we'll think of something. In the meantime, I'll go and grab the flashlights."

"I'll see if I can find Eugene," said Stan. "I want to take his camera. I want proof that we really saw Bigfoot."

"That's good thinking," said Stinky. "Just like the troop motto: Never Be Unprepared."

Stan couldn't find Eugene, but he borrowed the camera anyway. *It's for a good cause. I'm sure he won't mind,* he thought.

Before long, Stinky and Stan were on the path to the Twilight Cave.

"I can't believe we're going to try and rescue Penelope," said Stinky.

"Yeah," agreed Stan. "But no one else is, so it's down to us."

"Maybe after this, she'll be nicer to us at school," Stinky suggested.

The brothers looked at each other and shook their heads. "Nah," they said with a laugh.

"Stinky! Stan!"

The boys turned to see Tiffanie and Steffanie coming up the path.

"What happened? Where's your troop leader?" asked Stan.

"She didn't believe us," explained Tiffanie.

"Aw, man," said Stan. "Neither did ours."

There was only one thing left to do. The boys and girls would have to work together for the greater good . . . or at least for Penelope.

CHAPTER TEN
THE TWILIGHT CAVE

Stinky, Stan, Tiffanie, and Steffanie stood outside the Twilight Cave where they found *three* warning signs.

Stinky took a deep breath. "Ready, everyone?" he asked.

The others nodded hesitantly, turned on their flashlights, and they all headed into the dark, mysterious spooky cave.

The ground began to slope downward as the foursome weaved their way through

the long tunnels. Water dripped down from the cracks in the rock above their heads. The temperature dropped and everyone shivered a little.

"I can see how having Bigfoot's fur would come in handy," said Stinky.

"I agree," said Steffanie, rubbing her arms to get rid of her goose bumps.

The boys led the way, as the girls huddled together.

"AAAH!" Steffanie screamed.

"What is it? What's wrong?" exclaimed Stan, shining his flashlight in her direction. "Is it Bigfoot?"

"No," replied Steffanie. "It's a spider!"

Stan rolled his eyes. "Come on."

The group rounded a corner and came to a very narrow passageway. Stan got down on his knees and crawled through to the other side.

"I'm not going through there," insisted Steffanie, her arms folded. "I'm not getting dirty."

Stinky couldn't believe what he was hearing. "What did you expect? It's a *cave*. There's no maid service."

"Remember: Penelope is *your* friend, not ours," Stan called out from the other side.

Stinky agreed. "I'm sure she'd do the same for you. Now, come on."

Actually, Stinky doubted that Penelope would ever put anyone else first. But he kept this thought to himself. He knew he just had to say the right thing to get the girls through the hole.

Steffanie and Tiffanie got down on their hands and knees and crawled through the hole.

"That wasn't too horrible, was it?" Stinky asked when they made it out.

All he got back were steely glares from the girls.

"Okay, okay," said Stinky. "Let's just move on."

But the group didn't get far . . .

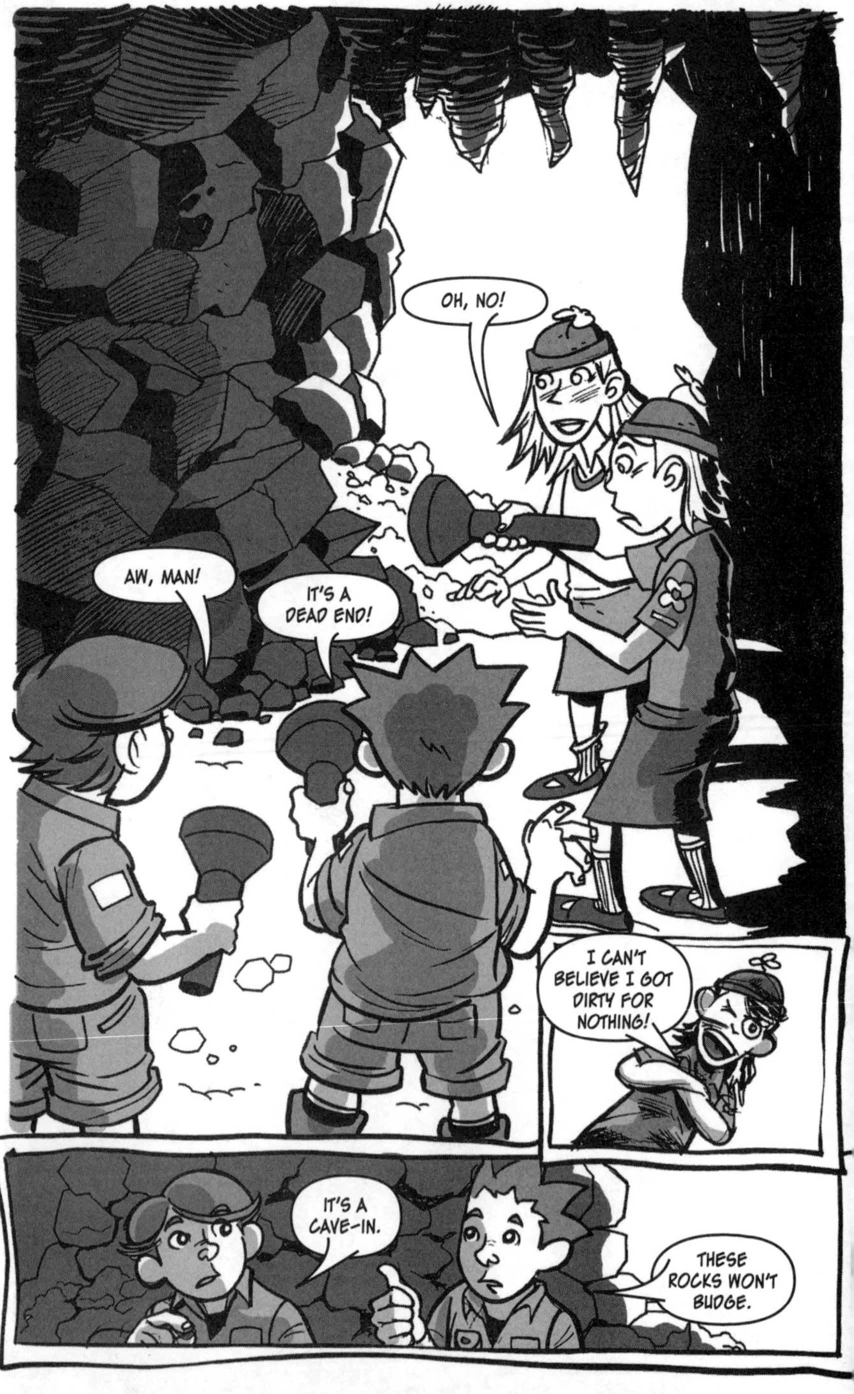
OH, NO!
AW, MAN!
IT'S A DEAD END!
I CAN'T BELIEVE I GOT DIRTY FOR NOTHING!
IT'S A CAVE-IN.
THESE ROCKS WON'T BUDGE.

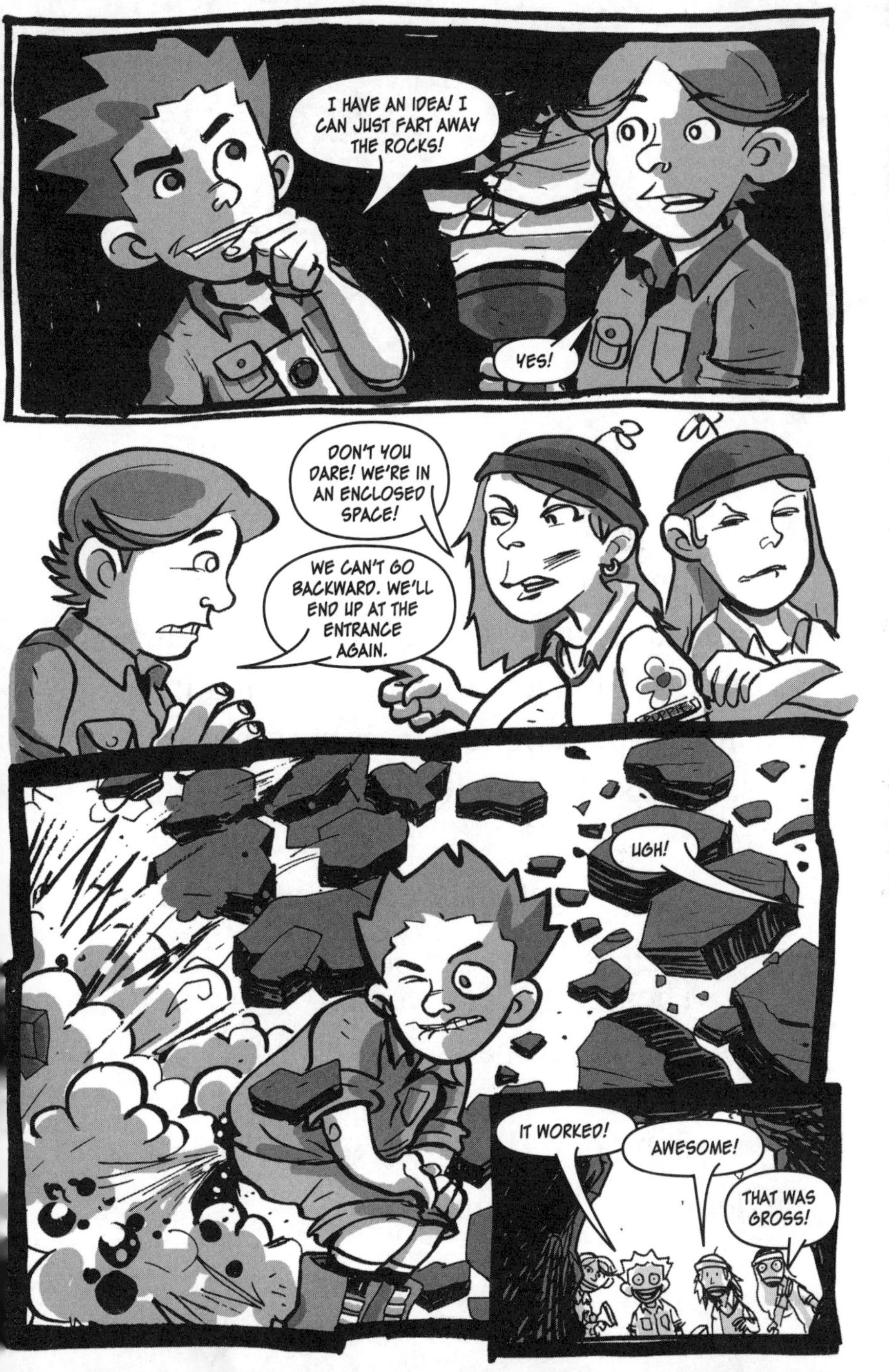
I HAVE AN IDEA! I CAN JUST FART AWAY THE ROCKS!
YES!
DON'T YOU DARE! WE'RE IN AN ENCLOSED SPACE!
WE CAN'T GO BACKWARD. WE'LL END UP AT THE ENTRANCE AGAIN.
UGH!
IT WORKED!
AWESOME!
THAT WAS GROSS!

Once the kids passed through the new hole, they weaved their way down a series of tunnels. Each one varied in size and shape. Along a narrow tunnel, they saw bats clinging to the ceiling with their feet.

"This is getting creepier and creepier," said Tiffanie.

Then things got worse.

The group had come to a fork in the path.

"Which way are we supposed to go?" demanded Steffanie.

"I don't know," said Stan. He shone
his flashlight down the path on the right
and then down the one on the left. They
both looked the same.

"We're going to have to split up,"
Stinky said.

The others looked at him in disbelief.
Split up?

"What if we get lost?" worried
Tiffanie.

"What if we get eaten?" asked Stan.

"What if we get eaten and then get
lost?" asked Steffanie.

"That doesn't make any sense," Stan to Steffanie.

"Oh . . . uh . . . whoops," said Steffanie.

"Guys, what choice do we have?" Stinky said. "Who knows how much danger Penelope is in? We don't want to waste any more time."

Everyone knew Stinky was right.

So the boys went one direction, and the girls went another, each pair secretly hoping the other pair would find Penelope—and Bigfoot—first.

CHAPTER ELEVEN

FIRE IN THE HOLE!

Stinky and Stan were walking for a while in the tunnel when they finally heard noises up ahead. They walked a little faster and eventually saw a flickering light, probably from a fire. When they were closer, the brothers ducked behind a very large boulder and peered out.

They weren't prepared for what they saw.

"Is that a—" said Stan, confused.

"That looks like—" Stinky said. He was astonished.

The boys were looking at a Bigfoot Wilderness Troop!

"That must be the troop leader," whispered Stan, pointing to the largest Bigfoot.

In the den, junior Bigfoots sat around a fire. They were furry and looked like the leader, except on a smaller scale. Stan noticed they were wearing sashes with patches on them over one shoulder, but he couldn't make out what the patches were.

The Bigfoot leader called to one of the junior Bigfoots.

"They speak English!" whispered Stinky.

"I know!" replied Stan. "Weird!"

The leader then praised the junior Bigfoot on earning his Human Patch.

That's right: a Human Patch! He had captured a human successfully.

That's when the boys saw Penelope. She was sitting in a corner of the cave, blindfolded and hugging her knees. She looked cold and scared.

Stinky and Stan ducked down behind the boulder to discuss what to do.

"I can't believe they have a Human Patch!" said Stan.

"I know. It's crazy!" said Stinky. "But we've got to concentrate on how to get Penelope out of there, without becoming Human Patches ourselves."

"I'm not sure we can do this," worried Stan. "I mean, there are so many more of them than us. And they're Bigfoots!"

Stinky looked squarely at his brother. "We can't give up now. We can do this. Remember: we're Buzzards!"

Stan took a deep breath.

"You're right. Let's come up with a plan."

"The good news is no one is guarding Penelope," said Stinky. "So, I think we should create a diversion and then go grab her."

"That sounds good," said Stan. "But for a diversion…hmmm…" He checked his pockets. He looked around on the ground. He looked up. Score! Stan grinned and pointed up to the ceiling.

Clinging to the cave ceiling were hundreds of bats.

"We can do a *Double Booty Bomber* and drive the bats into the Bigfoots' den," suggested Stan. "Then we'll sneak in and grab Penelope."

"Sounds perfect!" said Stinky. "Let's do it!"

Stan let out a loud fart and Stinky let out a smelly fart at exactly the same time.

The combination of smell and sound hit the bats and immediately woke them up. They rapidly flew to get away from it, flying right into the Bigfoots' den. The plan was underway . . .

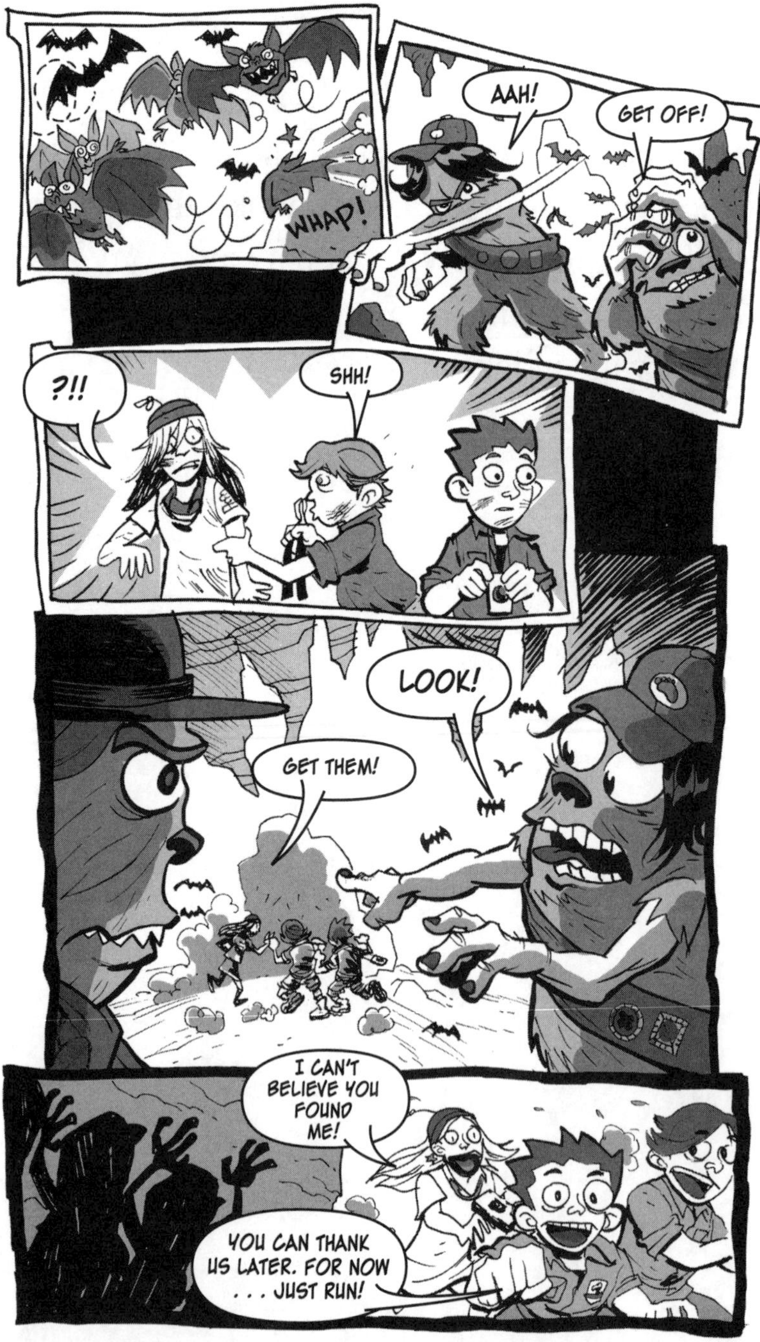
WHAP!
AAH!
GET OFF!
?!!
SHH!
LOOK!
GET THEM!
I CAN'T BELIEVE YOU FOUND ME!
YOU CAN THANK US LATER. FOR NOW . . . JUST RUN!

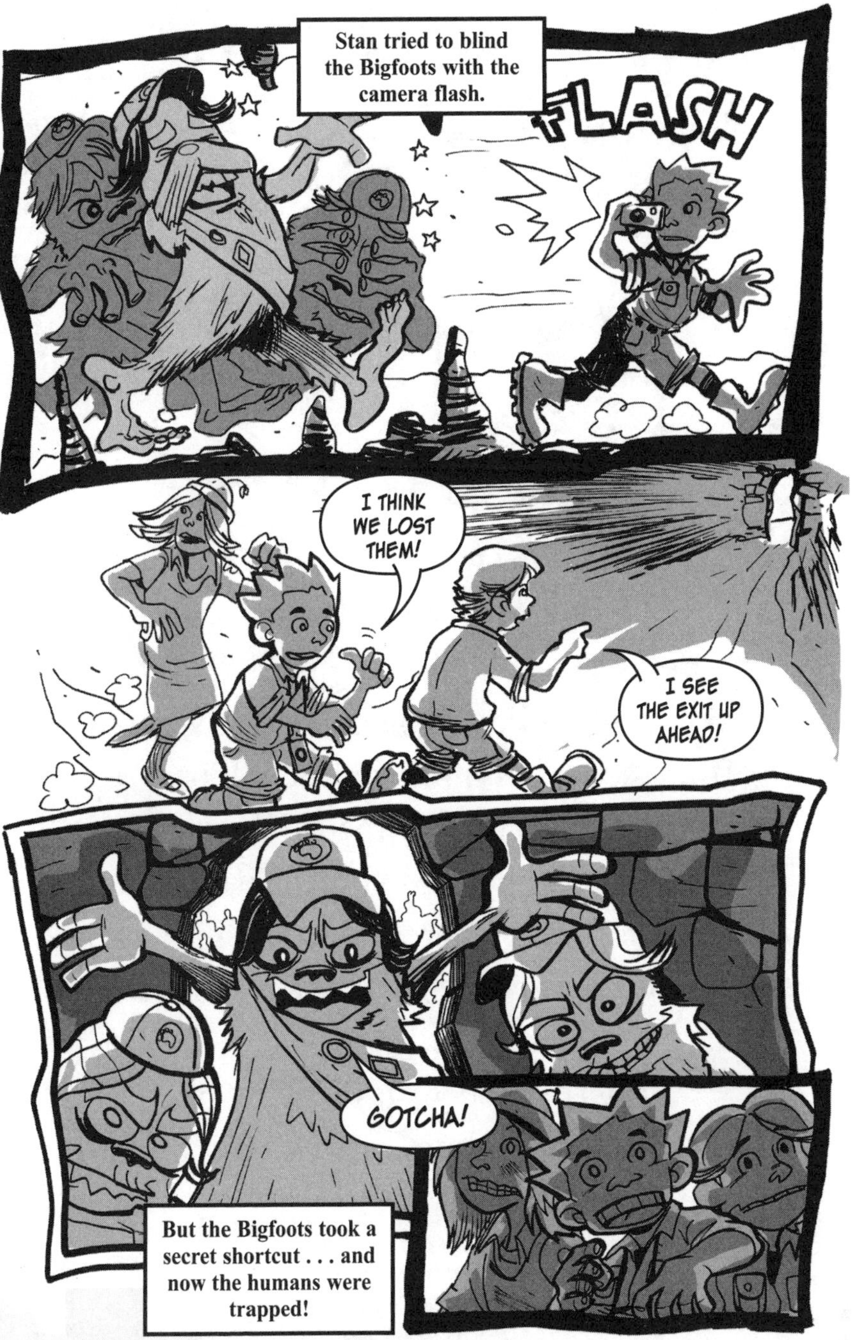
Stan tried to blind the Bigfoots with the camera flash.
FLASH
I THINK WE LOST THEM!
I SEE THE EXIT UP AHEAD!
GOTCHA!
But the Bigfoots took a secret shortcut . . . and now the humans were trapped!

CHAPTER TWELVE
PATCHING THINGS UP

"I can't believe you couldn't even pull off a rescue," complained Penelope.

She was back in the Bigfoots' den, alongside Stinky and Stan. Tiffanie and Steffanie were there, too, having been captured separately. A few Bigfoots were guarding them.

"You're complaining because we tried to rescue you?!" exclaimed Stinky.

"If you're going to rescue someone, you have to *actually* rescue them!" Penelope replied.

Stinky was fuming. "Fine! Next time, we'll just leave you—"

"Guys! Be quiet! We're about to be dinner!" said Stan.

"Stop bickering," ordered the Bigfoot leader in a deep, rumbling voice. Stinky, Stan, and Penelope immediately shut their mouths.

"Now, first of all, we're not going to hurt you," said the leader. "We are not as dangerous as you humans think."

All the humans heaved a sigh of relief.

"We are the oldest Bigfoot Wilderness Troop in the world," the leader explained. "Since you humans were constantly looking for us, setting traps for us, and taking our picture, we've been forced to live in caves and build secret passageways."

"Then why take the risk of leaving the cave by going out and capturing humans?" asked Stinky.

"Our troop members want their achievement patches, just like you," said the leader.

"A-ha!" Stan said. "We totally understand."

"But you have such weird patches," said Penelope. She saw one called Spot the Loch Ness Monster and another called Tame the Griffin.

"We could say the same about *your* patches," the Bigfoot leader replied.

Penelope gave a small smile. "Good point."

At that moment, some of the junior Bigfoots felt comfortable enough to go up to the boys and girls. Both the humans

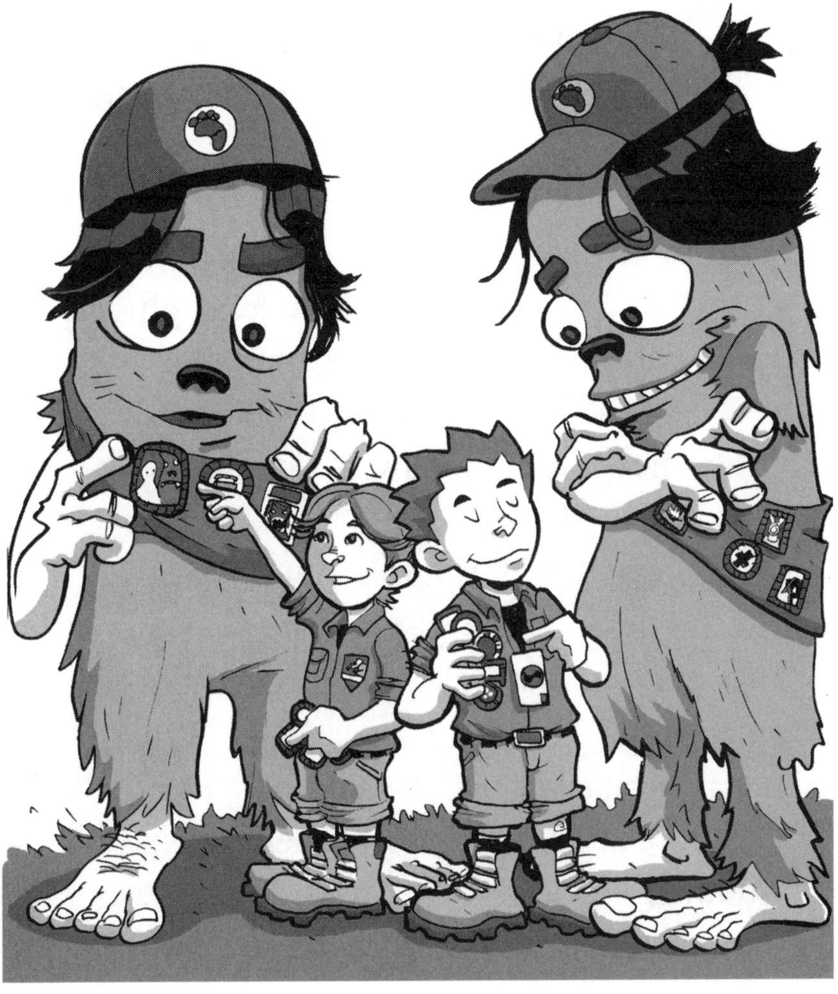

and the Bigfoots were curious about one another and soon discovered that they weren't as different as they thought.

"Hey, how do you know how to speak English?" Stinky asked one of the Bigfoots.

"The Internet," replied the junior Bigfoot.

"Ah," said Stinky. Sure enough, in one part of the cave was a computer!

"Some campers left it behind after they saw us and ran away," explained the Bigfoot.

Soon it was time to figure out what to do next. The Bigfoot leader explained to the humans the "catch-and-release program."

"Whenever one of the junior Bigfoots captures a human to earn their patch, the human is usually blindfolded. That way, when they are brought to our den, they

don't see where we live and our home
and future are safe. Then we bring them
back out of the cave afterward." He faced
Stinky and Stan. "But you have found our
home, learned our secrets, and that's a
whole different ball of fur."

Stinky and Stan looked at each other. A wave of worry washed over them. Were the Bigfoots planning on keeping them there forever so they wouldn't tell anyone else?

Just then, a glint caught Stinky's eye. It was the firelight reflecting off the camera around Stan's neck.

"Wait! I have an idea," said Stinky.

"Oh, great," chimed in Penelope. "Is it as good as your rescue plan?"

"That was uncalled for, young lady," said the Bigfoot leader.

Penelope opened her mouth to respond but nothing came out. She couldn't believe she was just scolded by a Bigfoot!

"What is your idea?" Stan asked his brother.

"We will give the camera to the Bigfoots," began Stinky.

"Huh?" said Stan. "What is that going to do?"

Stinky explained, "If the Bigfoots were able to just take a *picture* of a human, rather than capture one, maybe it would be enough proof to earn the Human Patch?"

"Hmmm," said the Bigfoot leader. "That's interesting . . ."

"That would also protect any future humans from getting captured," continued Stinky. "In return, all of us vow to keep you Bigfoots and your location a secret."

Stan and the girls nodded their agreement.

"Besides, no one will believe we found the Bigfoot den anyway," offered Stan. "Not to mention a whole Bigfoot troop!"

The Bigfoot troop voted and unanimously approved the idea.

"Awesome!" cheered Stan.

"Yeah!" said the girls.

The Bigfoot troop escorted the humans to the entrance of the Twilight Cave and said goodbye. The girls went back to their camp, and the boys headed toward theirs.

"Thanks for the camera," the Bigfoot leader called to Stan.

"No problem," Stan yelled back. "Thanks for the adventure!"

"Hey, isn't that Eugene's camera we just gave them?" Stinky said suddenly.

"Yup," said Stan. "I figured we'd just tell him a bear ate it."

Stinky laughed. "Good thinking. It's more believable than the truth!"

THE END

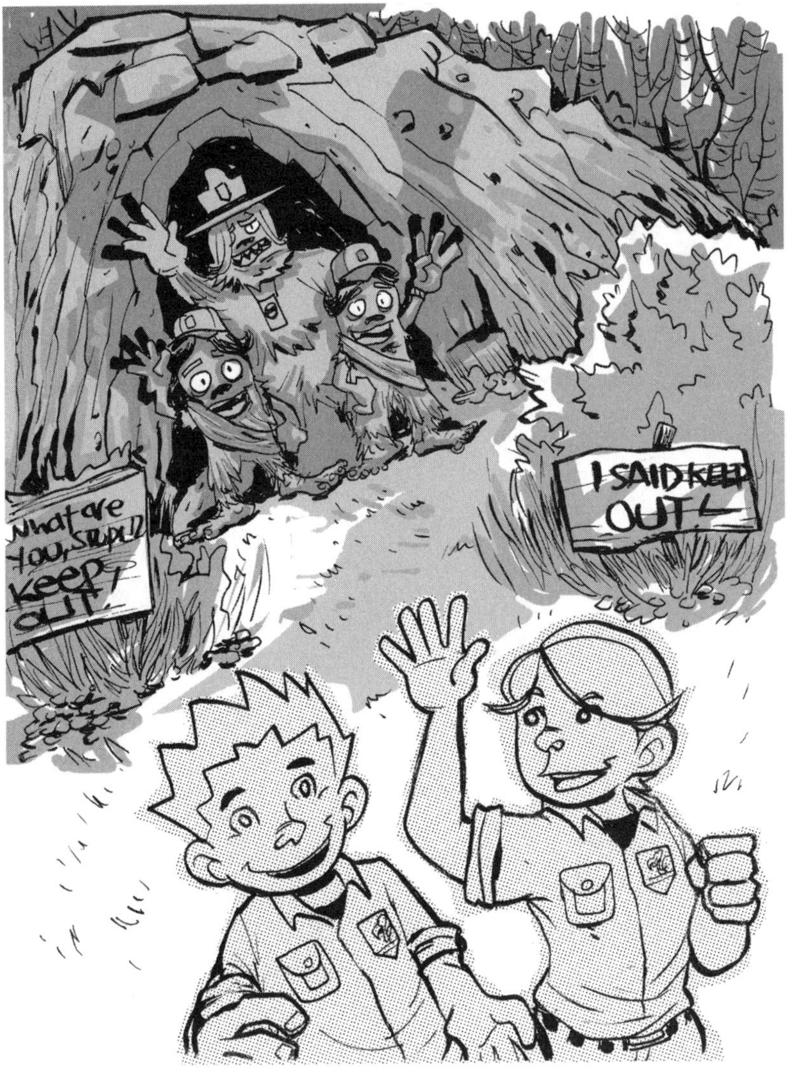
What are you, stupid? Keep out!
I SAID KEEP OUT!